NO!

I WON'T GO TO SCHOOL

TILBURY HOUSE PUBLISHERS
12 Starr Street, Thomaston, Maine 04861
800-582-1899 • www.tilburyhouse.com

Hardcover ISBN 978-088448-646-6

First hardcover printing April 2018

15 16 17 18 19 20 XXX 10 9 8 7 6 5 4 3 2 1

Library of Congress Control Number: 2018936801

English-language edition published by
arrangement with Base tres, www.base-tres.com

Cover and interior designed by Frame25 Productions

Printed in China

NO!

I WON'T GO TO SCHOOL

Alonso Núñez

Illustrations by Bruna Assis Brasil

Translated by Dave Morrison

TILBURY HOUSE PUBLISHERS, THOMASTON, MAINE

I know two letters,
the **N** and the **O**.
On the first day of school,
they spell a word:

NO!

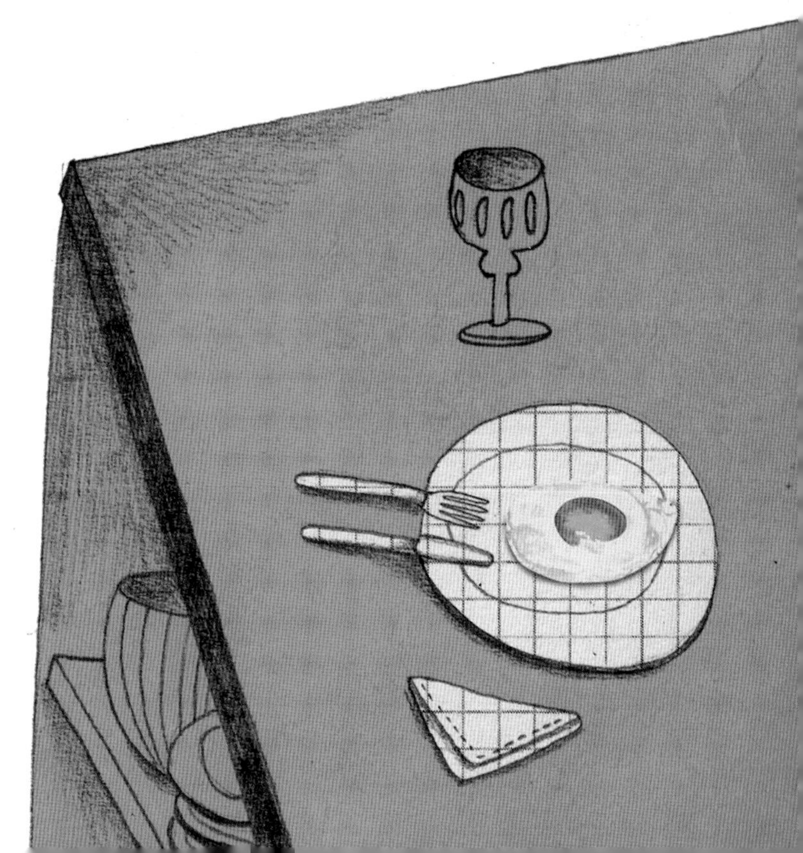

Mom says I'll make friends,
that the place is so cool,
that I'll learn new things,
that I'll really *like* school!

But I know she's lying
when she says I'll have fun.
I know school is awful.
I know when to run!

ACTORS ON ACTING

She says I'm going.
I say I won't go.
She says I will.
I say **N, O!**

The teacher's a monster
with big claws and four heads,
jaws that can crush you,
and eyes that turn red!

I'm not going to school.
I'm not going—

N, O!

Boys get in trouble
at every suggestion.
Girls know the answers
to all of the questions.

What a terrible place.
Am I going?

N! O!

Look at the time.
You can't be serious!
It's not even seven.
I think I'm delirious.

I'm running a fever.
I'm not going—

N!! O!!

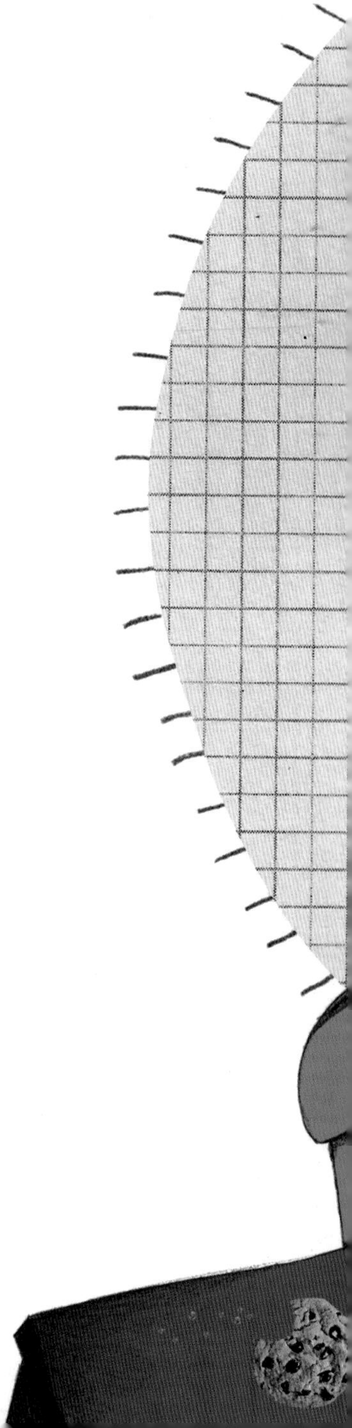

NG

This is getting me nowhere,
saying **N**, **O**, and **NO**.
Have they stopped working,
the **N** and the **O**?

Maybe Mom can't read
when the letters are small.
If I write my **NO** bigger,
will that help at all?

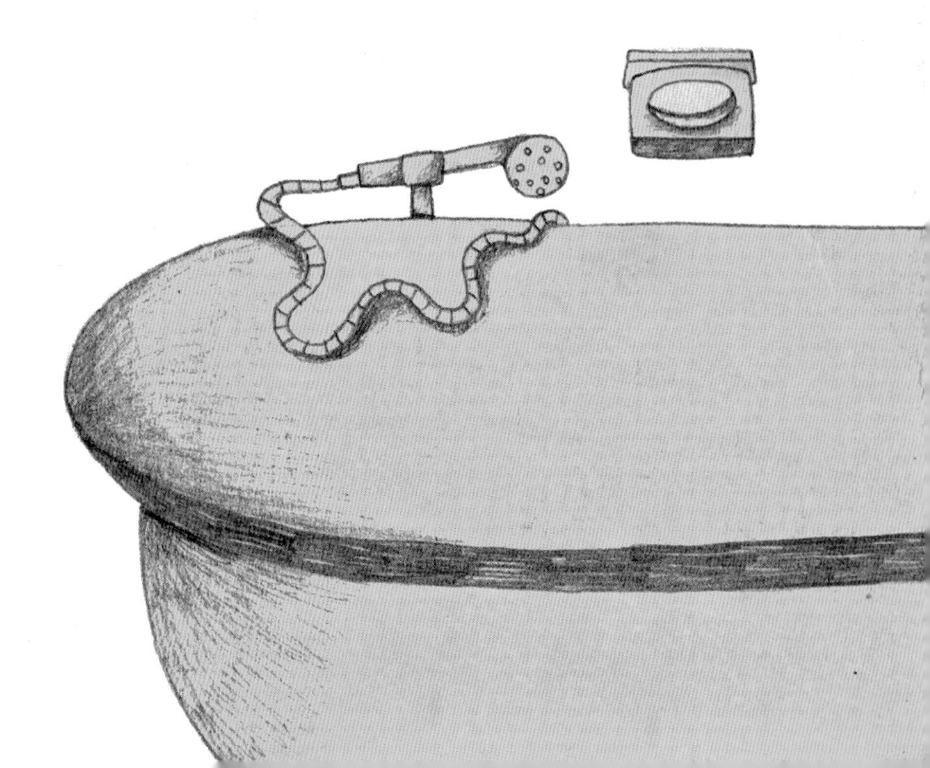

What's that yellow monster
that rumbles and rolls?
It's eating us kids—
it swallows us whole!

Now I'm in the belly
of this monstrous bus.
The driver's a zombie
who won't talk to us.

It's crowded with kids—
what a curious bunch!
A girl's singing show tunes;
a boy eats his lunch.

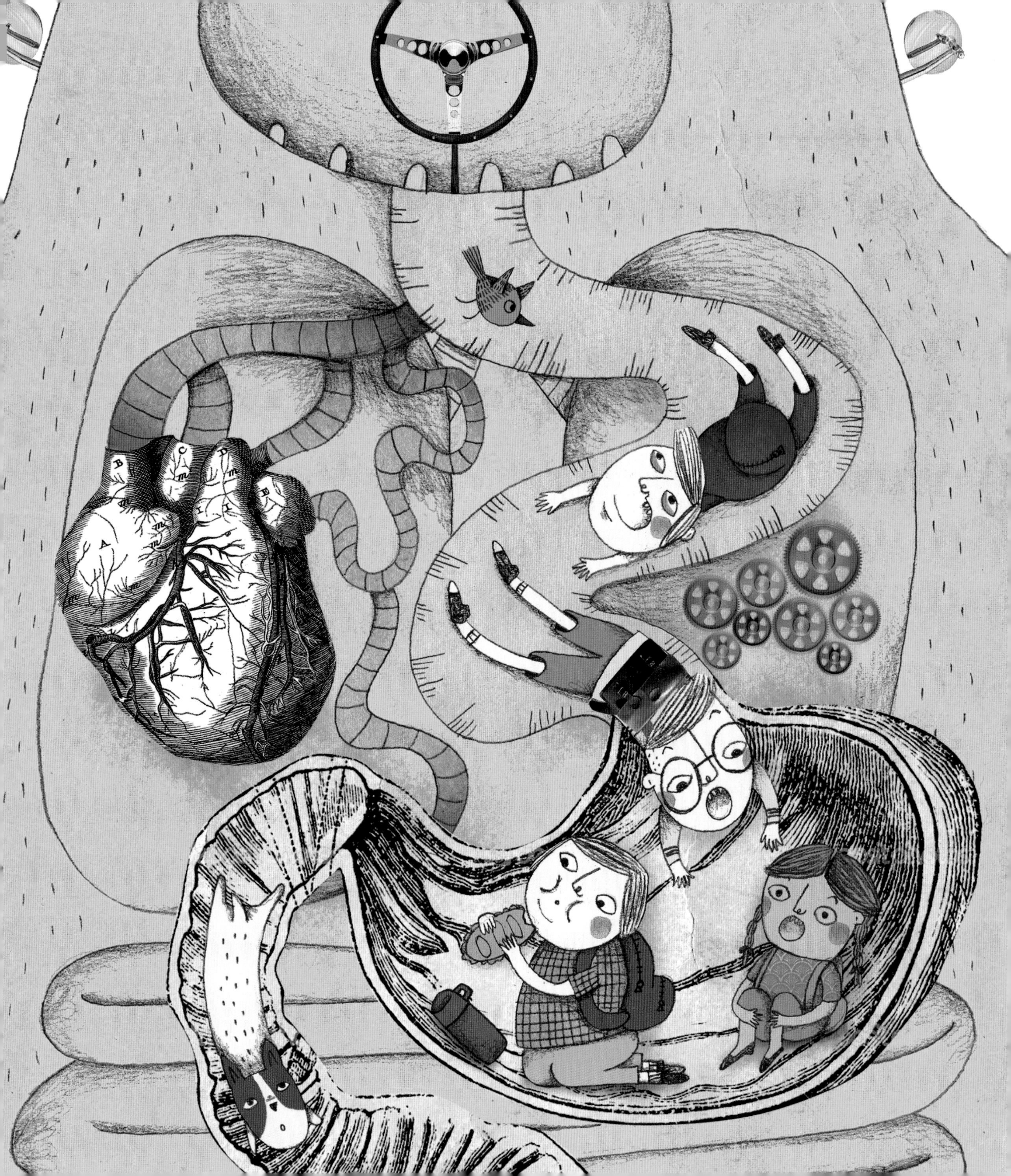

One boy chews his nails,
one girl cries with fright.
Those twins have green skin.
Something isn't quite right.

Now what is happening?
The monster goes slow.
It spits us out.
We're at school—oh, **NO!**

This place is a prison.
We all stand in line.
They'll chain us together.
We're all doing time!

The principal frowns.
His long mustache twitches.
He'll give us all shovels
and make us dig ditches.

A
C
D
E
F
L
M

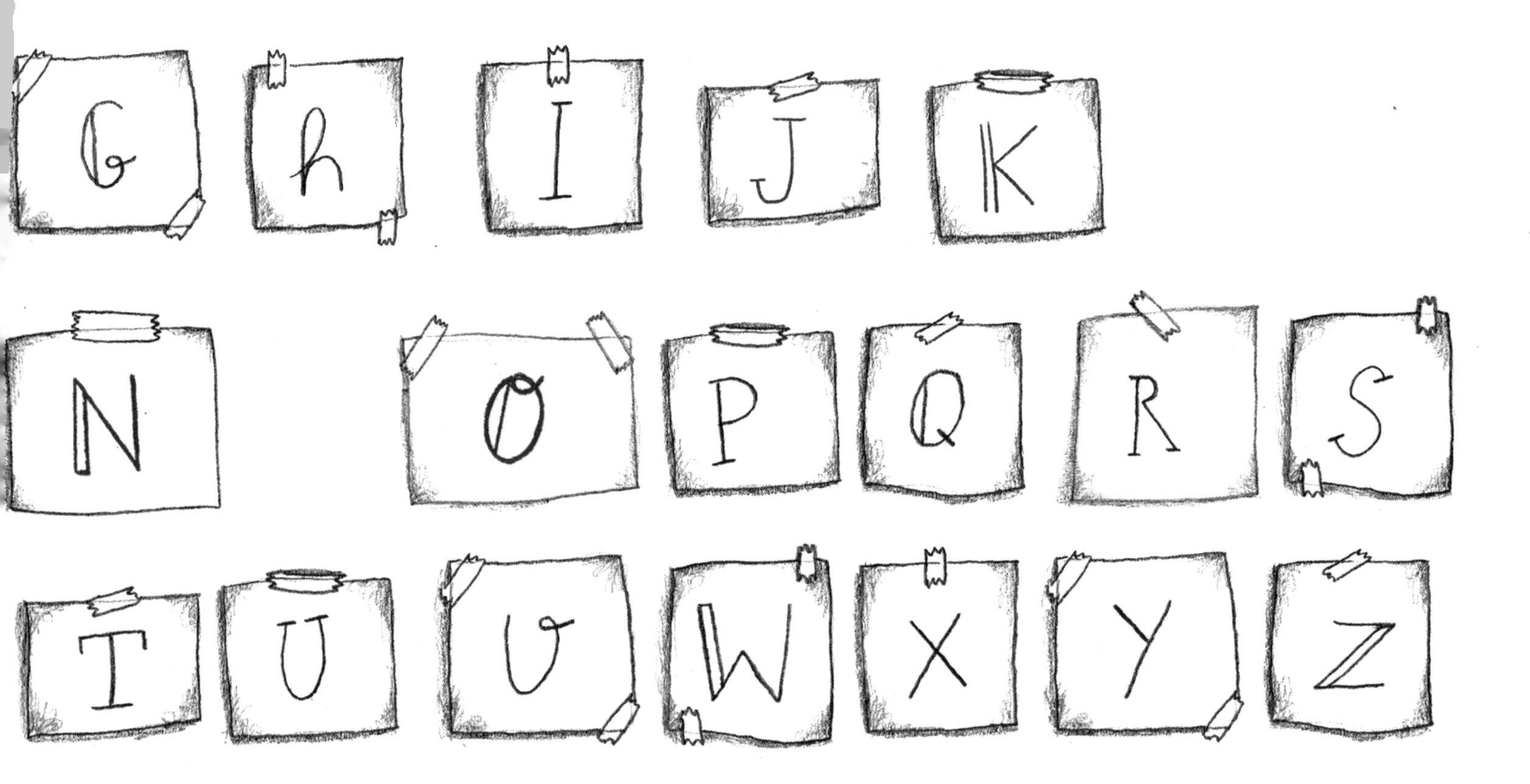

Instead we file in–
to the classroom we go!
On the wall with the letters
I see **N** and **O**.

Are they not going to eat us
or throw us in cells?
Is school not a dungeon?
Could this turn out well?

At the end of the day
with my things in my pack,
I return to my home,
shouting, "Hey Mom, I'm back!"

20
29

"There are lots of letters
besides **O** and **N**.
Numbers that go
from 1 up to 10.

"I made six new friends
and learned two Spanish words.
'Mamá' means Mom
and 'pájaro' means bird.

"I learned lots of things
that you may not know,
things way beyond
the **N** and the **O**."

29
ZAGAT

The teacher's not scary,
but patient and kind,
and if I make even more friends
that would be fine!

Tomorrow when the bus comes
and it's time to go,
maybe, just maybe
I won't say **N, O**.

I might not say no
but I might not say yes.
I really don't know.

It's anyone's guess.

ALONSO NÚÑEZ was born in 1969 in Mexico City, and his parents named him after the literary world's most beloved lunatic, Alonso el Bueno, better known as Don Quixote of La Mancha. He is the author of several bestselling children's books in Mexico, which have been translated to Chinese, Korean, and Portuguese. *NO!* is Alonso's first English-language children's book.

BRUNA ASSIS BRASIL was born in Curitiba, Brazil, in 1986. She majored in Journalism and Graphic Design, later specializing in Illustration, at the Escola de Disseny i Art in Barcelona. Bruna has illustrated more than 40 books and won the Jabuti Prize, Brazil's highest award for children's illustrations, in 2016. She also won the 2015 Açorianos Prize for Literature, and her work was selected in 2012 and 2016 for *Crescer* magazine's Thirty Best Children's Books of the Year in Brazil.

DAVE MORRISON is the author of twelve volumes of poetry, including *Clubland, Cancer Poems*, and *Psalms*.